MOUSE MATH™

# ALBERT'S AMAZING SNAIL

by **Eleanor May** • Illustratmon

THE KANE PRESS / NEW YORK

*For Renza, Marcello, and Valentina*
*—E.M.*

Text copyright © 2012 by Eleanor May
Illustrations copyright © 2012 by Deborah Melmon

Library of Congress Cataloging-in-Publication Data

May, Eleanor.
Albert's amazing snail / by Eleanor May ; illustrated by Deborah Melmon.
p. cm. — (Mouse math)
"With fun activities!"—Cover.
Summary: Albert the mouse tries to teach his new pet snail Flash how to do tricks and learns that patience can be a very good thing when it comes to snails. Introduces such position words as near and far, top and bottom, and on and off.
ISBN 978-1-57565-442-3 (pbk. : alk. paper) — ISBN 978-1-57565-443-0 (e-book) —
ISBN 978-1-57565-448-5 (library reinforced binding : alk. paper)
[1. Mice—Fiction. 2. Snails as pets—Fiction. 3. English language—Synonyms and antonyms—Fiction.] I. Melmon, Deborah, ill. II. Title.
PZ7.M4513Al 2012
[E]—dc23    2011048824

1 3 5 7 9 10 8 6 4 2

First published in the United States of America in 2012 by Kane Press, Inc.
Printed in the United States of America
WOZ0712

Book Design: Edward Miller

Mouse Math is a trademark of Kane Press, Inc.

Visit us online at **www.kanepress.com**

Like us on Facebook
facebook.com/kanepress

Follow us on Twitter
@KanePress

Dear Parent/Educator,

"I can't do math." Every child (or grownup!) who says these words has at some point along the way felt intimidated by math. For young children who are just being introduced to the subject, we wanted to create a world in which math was not simply numbers on a page, but a part of life—an adventure!

Enter Albert and Wanda, two little mice who live in the walls of a People House. Children will be swept along with this irrepressible duo and their merry band of friends as they tackle mouse-sized problems and dilemmas. (And sometimes *cat-sized* problems and dilemmas!)

Each book in the **MOUSE MATH**™ series provides a fresh take on a basic math concept. The mice discover solutions as they, for instance, use position words while teaching a pet snail to do tricks or count the alarmingly large number of friends they've invited over on a rainy day—and, lo and behold, they are doing math!

Math educators who specialize in early childhood learning used their expertise to make sure each title would be as helpful as possible to young kids—and to their parents and teachers. Fun activities at the end of the books and on our website encourage children to think and talk about math in ways that will make each concept clear and memorable.

As with our award-winning Math Matters® series, our aim is to captivate children's imaginations by drawing them into the story, and so into the math at the heart of each adventure. It is our hope that kids will want to hear and read the **MOUSE MATH** stories again and again and that, as they grow up, they will approach math with enthusiasm and see it as an invaluable tool for navigating the world they live in.

Sincerely,

Joanne Kane

Joanne E. Kane
Publisher

Check out these titles in
**MOUSE MATH**:

**The Right Place for Albert**
One-to-One Correspondence

**The Mousier the Merrier!**
Counting

**Albert's Amazing Snail**
Position Words

**Albert Keeps Score**
Comparing Numbers

And visit
www.kanepress.com/
mousemath.html
for more!

Albert was so excited he could hardly squeak.

"Look, Wanda!" he said. "I found a snail.
I've named him Flash. He's my new pet!
I'm going to teach him all kinds of tricks."

Albert's big sister, Wanda, looked at Flash.

"Can snails learn tricks?" she asked.

"Flash can," Albert said. "Flash is very smart.
You can see it in his eyes."

"Watch," Albert told her.
"Let's go, Flash!"

Albert scampered off.

6

Albert came back.

"Flash," he said. "When I say, 'Let's go,' you go **next to** me."

Wanda said, "Maybe you should teach him *stay*. I think Flash would be good at *stay*."

"I'll try *come*," Albert said.

Albert ran across the yard. He turned and clapped his paws.

"Flash! *Come!*"

Wanda looked at her watch.
"I think this is going to take awhile," she said.

Albert said, "You have to be patient when you train a pet."

Wanda went inside.

Albert's friend Leo came by.
"Why are you just sitting there?" Leo asked.

"I'm not just sitting here," Albert said.
"I'm training my pet snail."

"Oh!" Leo looked across the yard at Flash.
"Isn't he a little **far** away?"

"I'm teaching him to come," Albert explained.
"He's **far** away now, but when he comes,
he will be **near**."

Leo sat down **beside** Albert. They waited.

"Once I read a book about snails," Leo told Albert. "It said that wherever snails go, they leave a trail of slime. Does your snail leave a trail of slime?"

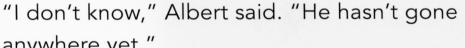

"I don't know," Albert said. "He hasn't gone anywhere yet."

Leo yawned.

"Maybe it would help if we did a few tricks," Albert said. "To show Flash how it's done."

"Watch this, Flash!" Albert said.
"I crawl **in** one end of the hollow log—"

"—and **out** the other end."

"Look, Flash!" Albert said. "I'm **on top of** this pile of pinecones!"

"Whoops. Now I'm **at the bottom of** the pile."

Leo climbed **on** a sunflower. "Watch me balance on one foot!" he said to Flash. "Can you do that?"

Albert said, "Leo, he's a snail. He only *has* one foot."

"Oh," Leo said. "Right. I forgot."
He jumped **off**.

Leo scampered up a tree.
"Look, Flash! I go **under** this branch—"

"—and then **over** the top!"

"I can hide **behind** this rock!" Albert said.

Leo said, "I can stand **in front of** it and do a crazy dance!"

"What in the world are you doing?" Wanda asked.

Albert and Leo looked at Wanda.
Albert said, "We're showing Flash some tricks."

"Well, you need to come inside now,"
Wanda told him. "Dinnertime."

Albert gave Flash a fresh green leaf.
"Practice your tricks!" he said. "Tomorrow you
can show us what you've learned."

First thing the next morning, Albert ran outside.
He couldn't wait to see how his pet snail was
doing with his tricks.

Soon Wanda came outside.
"Albert, what's wrong?" she asked.

"Flash hasn't learned a single trick! He hasn't
budged at all!" Albert sniffled. "Maybe he isn't
as smart as I thought."

Wanda put her arm around Albert.

Then she pointed at the ground. "What's that?"

Albert looked. It was . . .

"A trail of slime!" Albert said, jumping up.

"The slime goes **in** one end of the log," Wanda said.

"And **out** the other end!" Albert exclaimed.
"Wanda, do you know what this means?"

"It means that I'm not going in that log,"
Wanda said.

"No!" Albert said. "It means *Flash did a trick!*"

Albert followed the trail of slime.
"I see slime here too! Flash was **on top of** the pinecones!"

"And **at the bottom**," Wanda said.

"Flash was **on** the sunflower," Wanda said.
"And then he got **off**."

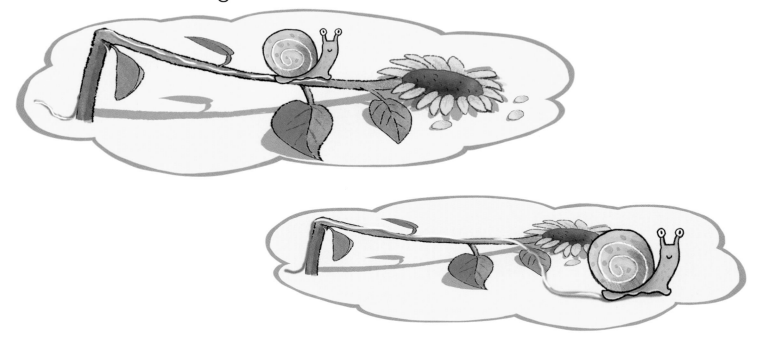

Albert scrambled up the tree. "Flash went
**under** the branch and **over** the top!"

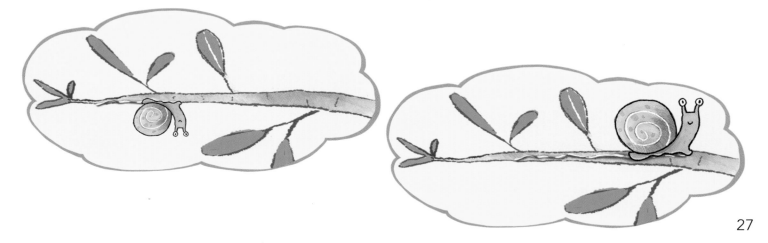

"Then he went **behind** the rock," Wanda said.

Albert beamed. "And here he is **in front of** it!"

"I knew you were smart, Flash!" Albert said.
"I knew you could learn tricks!"

Wanda smiled. "Albert, you were right.
Training a pet just takes patience . . .
lots and lots of patience."

Albert smiled too. "Just wait till you see what I teach him next!"

*Albert's Amazing Snail* supports children's understanding of **position words**, an important topic in early math learning. Use the activities below to extend the math topic and to reinforce children's early reading skills.

##  ENGAGE

▶ Invite children to look at the cover as you read the title. Talk about what it means to be "amazing." Ask: *How do you think Albert feels about his snail? What things do you know about snails?* Talk about the illustration on the cover. *What is Albert's snail doing?*

## LOOK BACK

▶ Re-read the story aloud. As you read, point to the illustrations and ask questions such as: *Where is Leo?* (Possible answer: Leo is **beside** Albert.) *Where is Albert? Flash?* Encourage children to reply using position words.

## TRY THIS!

▶ Have children look at each drawing below as you read the sentence aloud. Read aloud the words in the Word Bank. Help children choose the position word that best fits each sentence. (Note: You may wish to make word strips using the position words.)

---

**WORD BANK**

inside   in front of   behind   on   under

---

The ladybug is _____ the grass.

The toadstools are _____ the log.

Fred is _____ the cookie jar.

The mouse is _____ the trash can pedal.

Ronald is _____ the cuckoo clock.

## 🐭 THINK!

Children will have fun coming up with silly sentences for their Position Word Booklets.

▶ Prepare booklets of 4 to 12 pages each. On each page, write a position word from the list below.

▶ Go to www.kanepress.com/mousemath-positionwords.html and print out the Picture Bank. Have children color the pictures, cut them out, and place them on the table or desk. (Alternatively, you may have children cut out pictures from magazines.)

▶ Direct children to the first page in their booklets. Read the position word aloud: for example, the word **beside**. Then say: *Choose two pictures and glue them down, one* **beside** *the other*. Continue until children complete their booklets.

▶ Encourage each child to make up silly sentences using his or her pictures and position words. (For instance, "The broccoli is **beside** the igloo!")

---

**POSITION WORDS**
far   near   beside   above   below
in front of   behind   on   next to   between   under   over

---

◆ **FOR MORE ACTIVITIES** ◆
visit www.kanepress.com/mousemath-activities.html